Ron Mueller

White Swan and Quiet Pheasant

By: *Ron Mueller*

Around the World Publishing, LLC
Cincinnati, Ohio

This story is a work of fiction. Names, characters, places, and incidents either are products of the author's imagination or are used fictitiously. Any resemblance to actual events or locales or persons, living or dead, is entirely coincidental.

White Swan and Quiet Pheasant ©

ISBN 13: 978-1-68223-407-5

Distributed by Ingram
Cover Picture by Hien Mueller
Cover Design By: Ron Mueller

The Stories of Taelo are set in the distant past, long before the time currently given as to when people migrated into the western hemisphere.

This is purposely done since the stories are meant to engage the reader in a story and not relate exact history.

The adventures of Taelo and Golden Hawk provide the backdrop for stories featuring the values of treating others as you wish to be treated, of responsibility, integrity, honesty and of contribution, and the joy of learning.

Ron Mueller

ℰ *Dedicated to: My White Swan: Hien* ℰ

Ron Mueller

White Swan and Quiet Pheasant

*T*he Elk Clan had traveled to a new world. It had endured a rigorous journey across dangerous glaciers, ice cold waters, mountains, and ferocious bears. They had established themselves in a new world. Through hard work they flourished.

They had constantly been pushed south by the brutal winters and had subdivided into multiple sub-clans. There were seven "Elk" clans. White Swan was a member of the Elk Horn Clan. Its traditional leaders treated the women as their property. This was something that White Swan and her sister Quiet Pheasant railed against.

The clan's prosperity meant that there was no reason to question the culture it practiced.

White Swan, stubborn and hardheaded, struggled accepting her role in a world ruled by the men that surrounded her.

She looked into the placid water at the reflection of her sister Quiet Pheasant. She recognized her younger sister as a person with a similar attitude and with a quiet conviction as strong as hers that they would not bend to such a situation. Her sister was the one that listened deeply and then later shared her insights.

The two were just twelve moons apart in age. They would spend endless amounts of time discussing how they could influence the decisions of their parents, their parent's friends, and their own constituency. They were determined to change their society.

White Swan's eyes lifted and took in the white capped mountains with their peaks lifting high above the broken layer of white clouds.

The sun was bright, and its warming rays warmed the back of her neck as she stayed kneeling at the water's edge.

Clear, early mornings such as this were rare.

White Swan turned her eyes once again to her sister and admired her slender figure. They were very much the same.

1

Winter had been hard but the two had proved to be good hunters of small game. They had rebelled against staying in the camp as the other young women did. They had consistently brought in enough small game that the family always had a solid evening meal.

Their parents accepted their wandering ways and gave them the freedom to do so. Both of them knew that their daughters were not to be contained.

White Swan endured the bullying taunts of the younger men and quite openly returned the taunts by noting the weakness of those teasing her.

She ignored the stern looks from both the older men and women.

She was constantly on the lookout for ways to respond in unexpected ways.

The most troubling was when White Swan overheard one of the elders speaking to her father about doing a better job at controlling his daughters. Quiet Pheasant overheard the same warning. The two discussed this and what they might do to maintain their freedom to do what they wanted to do.

There seemed to be no direct way.

They came up with an approach that would serve them well throughout their lifetime. They began with their parents, prepared a celebration dinner, and let them know what great parents they were.

Their mother pulled them aside and asked what they were up to.

White Swan replied that they were only treating everyone the way they wished to be treated.

Quiet Pheasant's assurance made their mother smile.

"I will help the two of you," their mother said with a smile. She too knew the frustration of fitting into the hard work of the camp while the young men went off on their hunting adventures.

The change in their behavior at first yielded a positive response but several of the older members of the leadership team continued to rail against the fact that the two were not engaged in the same manner as the other young women.

White Swan and Quiet Pheasant continued their excursions out into the wilderness. They roamed the hills like the tomboys they were.

Their father taught them how to hunt and how to protect themselves. He was very proud of his daughters capabilities.

He showed them not only how to protect themselves from the wild animals with spears and a small stone hammer, but also from other humans.

White Swan listened to her father as he showed her how to use the power of a larger opponent to overcome him. This was an ancient art that had been passed down to him from his father and grandfather.

The direct support of their father was important to both she and Quiet Pheasant.

Quiet Pheasant commented later that their father was worried about what some of the elders might do because they were breaking the unwritten rules of the clan.

Everyday White Swan and Quiet Pheasant would go out to a secluded location and practice what their father had taught them. It was not long before White Swan was certain that she and Quiet Pheasant could beat any of the young men in a one-on-one fight.

They did their victory dance in celebration of the praise they received from both their father and mother.

They continued to practice their self-defense and they continued to hunt.

They were now on a hunt and were now on the attack.

White Swan felt the early morning sun on her neck. Her breathing was deep and steady. Her heartbeat was a deep steady rhythm. Her legs were taking long smooth strides. Her feet barely touched the ground. She felt the pure energy rise into her mind. She knew she was in the other world where she could do anything and be anyone.

Her eyes were glued to the body of the large woolly buffalo racing at top speed. She was running at its side. She kept the young bull running away from the herd.

She was slowly moving him farther away and up toward the thick pine covered hills that surrounded the long flat valley.

The sky above was a clear blue, the wind was in her face. It was a glorious day.

Out to her left she looked at her sister. Quiet Pheasant carried a spear in each hand and her arms pumped back and forth as if she was using them to power her swiftly moving legs. Her feet seemed to barely touch the ground as she fluidly kept pace with the swiftly moving young buffalo that she had selected for herself.

They were duplicate images. Boths racing next to young buffaloes that were headed toward the forest.

White Swan smiled and turned her attention back to her buffalo. She was confident they both would be taking the humps of these young bulls as rewards to their mother.

Her long black hair flew parallel to the ground as she picked up the pace. It was almost time to bring down the young bull. White Swan judged the distance to the edge of the woods. She would put down her bull at the base of the tree that she would use to hang him up in.

Guide my hands she thought up to the ancestors of old. She then raced out ahead of the young bull. She had carried the spear in her right hand with the head pointed behind her. This was the way the old hunter had said it should be done. Once she was ahead of the bull, she planted the butt of the spear in the ground and simultaneously placed the head just inside of the bulls left front leg.

The bull ran up onto the spear and slid on his knees as his heart stopped.

She stopped. She glanced to her left where she made eye contact with Quiet Pheasant who had done the same and was looking to her right.

Both were prepared to use their other spear should it be necessary. It was not. Their first spears went almost halfway into the young bull's chest. Their front legs had buckled. They had died instantly and appeared to be bowing to the tree that stood only a body length away.

White Swan again looked at Quiet Pheasant. Simultaneously they both let out their adrenalin powered cries of victory and raced toward each other and did a whooping dance. They had talked about this moment for most of the winter months. They had practiced running full speed carrying their spears. They had asked about hunting buffalo and listened to all the old warriors as they explained how to hunt buffalo.

Only their father had described the technique they had just used.

"Only the fastest hunters and only those with enough stamina to run their buffalo long and hard can hunt the buffalo and never throw their spear. They do not need strength.

They need speed and stamina.

Both of you can do it," he had explained with a twinkle in his eye.

He knew what White Swan and Quiet Pheasant wanted. He wished he could be with them to witness their success.

White Swan had thanked him and after a few more question, she and Quiet Pheasant had started their preparations.

Their preparation had been rewarded.

"One for each of us. Now the hard work begins. We need to get them off the ground where the wolves and bears cannot get to them. Let's go get our gear and get them skinned and the meat into the trees," White Swan said once the two of them had recovered from the run and the excitement of the kill.

"You know that now the elders will really be upset about our behavior," Quiet Pheasant commented.

"Oh, this will raise many questions and will surely get us into trouble. How could two weak women dare to hunt the buffalo," White Swan responded in a deep voice and then she let out a laugh and enjoyed the fact that Quiet Pheasant was laughing with her.

"Yes, father will have his hands full dealing with the elders, but he will be laughing with us, and mother will help by cooking a dinner for all the elders," Quiet Pheasant added.

White Swan and Quiet Pheasant managed to get the buffalo skinned and the majority of the meat hung up into the high branches of the tree. They moved all the scraps away from where they had hauled the meat into the high branches.

They harnessed themselves to the travois loaded with the two shoulder humps, two hides, the tongues, hearts, livers, and kidneys of the young buffaloes.

They would return to the camp well after dark. Their load was all they could handle. It was much harder than they had imagined it would be.

"Well, I was worried that my two daughters had met their fate," their father spoke up as he met them about halfway back to camp. He took in contents of the travois.

"Oh, this will be so much fun. My two daughters have just passed the challenge of becoming hunters and young warriors.

This after I agreed to make sure you behaved as appropriate for young women of the clan," he continued as he gave them both a hug.

"I will pull the travois into camp. You two go to the river and clean up. I am sure your mother will have some of the hump meat prepared by the time you get done," their father directed as they came within sight of their lodge.

His pulling in a travois loaded with some hides would seem normal. He had decided that confronting the issue the next day would make it easier.

White Swan was surprised by her father's enthusiastic headlong attack on the customs of the clan. He insisted that she and Quiet Pheasant be recognized as warriors and hunters of the clan.

To her amazement the elders yielded to giving them the title of hunters but would not yield to giving them the distinction of being warriors.

The autumn clan meeting was fast approaching. The clan meetings were a time of celebration and of romance.

White Swan had her eyes on a specific young warrior and hunter in the Elk Hide Clan named Grey Fox Running.

She mentioned this to Quiet Pheasant who replied that his buddy, Red Oak was of interest to her.

"We need to get them out alone and see what they are made of. I do not want to be a servant or maid to any man," White Swan commented.

"Let's take them on a hunt and see how they react when we out hunt them," Quiet Pheasant suggested.

In the sun cycles leading up to their departure for the Elk Clan gathering, White Swan put all of her talent to work.

She would give her mate to be gifts he would be proud to wear. She made a vest and a pair of footwear. She was not sure of the foot size and left them partially undone so she could custom fit them.

Quiet Pheasant followed her lead and did the same. Their vests were similar, but the fur trim and the front fastenings were unique in each case.

White Swan used the toenails from a dire wolf that went through an opposing leather loop whereas Quiet Pheasant used hand carved pieces of red oak wood that went through slits on the opposing side of the vest.

White Swan used grey fox fur for her trim, while Quiet Pheasant used red fox fur for the trim. The smooth, soft finish of the leather, the minimal but distinctive trim, the rabbit fur lining on the inside all combined to make the gifts unique and valuable.

They both wanted to display their skill at providing clothing and they planned to later show off their cooking skills.

"I see you have your eyes set on some young men," their mother commented when she saw what White Swan and Quiet Pheasant were doing.

5

"Make sure of the character of the man, do not go only on his looks," was her only comment.

"Is it OK if he is also good looking," White Swan said with a chuckle?

She got a nod and a smile from her mother.

Two sun cycles later the Elk Horn Clan departed for the Clan gathering. The clan was hoping to be the first to arrive. A few sun cycles later the valley came into sight.

White Swan and Quiet Pheasant pulled their travois as the Elk Horn Clan crested the hill.

The oblong valley bordered by the thick stand of brown trunked, dark green pine, stretched out before them. At the far end the crystal-clear waters of a lake reflected the blue of the sky and the yellow of the weeping willow trees that graced its banks. The thick grasses and drying flower stems undulated, as the wind at their back passed the clan and seemed to massage the tall thick mass of grass that spread before them.

They were the first clan to arrive. They would have the choice of sites. White Swan let out a sigh of relief. The burden of carrying water would be easier. She looked over at Quiet Pheasant and they both gave a knowing smile.

All the sub clans of the Elk Clan camped on one side of the lake. Every season one clan stayed behind to ensure the valley was put back to its natural state. The stones for the fire pits and the stones used to hold down the lodge hides were gathered and put in small separate piles.

White Swan and Quiet Pheasant put all their effort into getting their campsite established. They gathered and positioned the rocks for the fire pit. They placed the stones around the base of their family lodge.

They put out the boundary markers.

Once their camp was complete, they disappeared to scout out the valley, the forest, and the other side of the low mountains.

They traveled a path they knew well in a steady jog. The two knew every trail, every major outcropping, and every bend. In the past, they had been to the head of the stream feeding the lake. This valley was theirs. They knew every major feature.

Periodically they would launch their small spears and a rabbit would meet its end. These they prepared for their lunch or dinner. White Swan had let her parents know that they would be back late or in the morning. Their goal was to scout out the game on the other side of the mountains. They were looking for buffalo.

They needed to test out the young men they had set their eyes on and had decided to take them on a hunt.

A few days later Quiet Pheasant tapped White Swan on the shoulder and pointed to the arriving clan. The Elk Hide Clan leader carried his spear with its distinctive red leather piece of Elk Hide high in the air as the clan entered camp.

White Swan listened to the song being chanted and sung by the on-coming clan.

"I will need to change that if I ever go into that clan," she quietly said to Quiet Pheasant.

"I agree but our quests seem to be enjoying their part in singing it," Quiet Pheasant replied.

White Swan and Quiet Pheasant walked by as the Elk Hide Clan organized their camp site. There were many young women coming of age. Competition for their young men was going to be high. White Swan had decided they would make immediate contact with their two young warriors.

White Swan's and Quiet Pheasant had gentle totem, but they were fierce competitors, and they were non-traditional. Let the beauties of the clan wait for their suitors to come to them. White Swan was going to capture hers while the others waited.

White Swan waited until the two were walking toward the upstream crossing where the small river fed the lake. She then approached them. Quiet Pheasant was at her side.

After some small talk and greetings, White Swan suggested they go and hunt a buffalo together.

The unusual suggestion stopped the conversation in its tracks.

She let the silence hang and returned a steady gaze back at the surprised Grey Fox Running.

Quiet Pheasant was doing the same with Red Oak.

The two young men looked at each other and with a nod they seemed to agree, and both smiled and accepted the invitation with the simple question, When?

White Swan suggested they leave early the next morning. They would meet at the spot they were on, just before sunrise.

She and Quiet Pheasant turned and walked back to their camp and shared the news with their parents.

"Don't scare those two young men," their mother commented when she learned of the upcoming hunt.

"Yes, I am getting too old to hunt for two mate-less women," their father commented as he chuckled.

"We will know by tomorrow night whether you have two mate-less daughters or two handsome new members of our family," White Swan replied.

That evening she and Quiet Pheasant danced the same victory dance they had done when they killed their first buffalo.

Now they would see if they could get a mate by sundown the following day.

Once White Swan and Quiet Pheasant had departed, Red Oak and Grey Fox Running were left standing looking at the two beauties that were walking away. They were somewhat disoriented.

"Did we just agree to go buffalo hunting with two very good-looking women," Red Oak commented as he shook his head?

All he could remember was gazing into the depth of Quiet Pheasant's dark black eyes.

"Yes, we leave before sunrise in the morning. Let's go get ready. I am not sure how we will hunt together. This should be one of the more interesting hunts we go on. I am not sure what or who is hunting or being hunted," Grey Fox Running replied as he remembered the honey-colored eyes that had penetrated his soul.

Grey Fox Running spent the rest of the evening replaying the encounter he had experienced with White Swan.

The next morning White Swan and Quiet Pheasant were waiting for Grey Fox Running and Red Oak. After a quick good morning White Swan led the group on a steady jogging pace along the almost invisible trail across the mountain.

The grey of early morning, the mist hanging low against the mountain and the quiet of the thick forest of leafless maples and dark green pine encouraged and enriched the quiet the four were sharing.

The sun slowly dispersed the mist and began to warm the air. The awakening of the morning seemed to draw out the low melodic chant she and Quiet Pheasant always shared as they jogged.

They harmonized and when one took the pitch up the other would go in the opposite direction. Soon all four were harmonizing together.

White Swan listened and smiled as Grey Fox Running and Red Oak took up the chant. They added depth and resonance.

She thought that the four sounded good together.

Then ahead the sea of bison lay before them. White Swan did not at first see them. They seemed to be the brown floor at the bottom of the mountain. Then her mind interpreted the scene, and she realized the herd went out as far as the eye could see into the dark blue cloudless horizon beyond.

She thanked the Ancients for providing the buffalo.

She stopped at the edge of the forest. The buffalo herd was no more than a few hundred feet away.

"Let's talk about how we will get our buffalo. We will only kill one. Quiet Pheasant and I will select a young bull, bring him to you, and drop him at your feet. If we miss you will get your turn. If we are successful you will do the skinning and prepare a travois to carry it back to the valley," White Swan said quietly.

"Why only one," both Red Oak and Grey Fox Running asked?

"Because we will need to carry everything we kill back across the mountain to the valley," Quiet Pheasant replied.

White Swan watched as the two men looked at each other.

"What more could we ask for than to have the buffalo delivered to us at our feet," Red Oak replied with a smile.

"Those two seem to have the guidance of the ancestors. They move so smoothly and effortlessly," Grey Fox Running commented as he watched White Swan point to the buffalo she had picked out.

The two exchanged comments about the ease and relaxed way the two young women were working together.

Red Oak wondered whether they be would strong enough to drive their spears into the bull for the kill?

White Swan took the side closest to the herd and Quite Pheasant paralleled her on the outside. Together, slowly with an ease that defied the situation they eased the young bull away from the edge of the herd and had it moving in an almost straight line toward where Grey Fox Running and Red Oak stood silently watching.

White Swan vocalized a sharp yell and was immediately joined by Quite Pheasant as the Bull began to run.

It was then that both Grey Fox Running and Red Oak noticed the inner spears each young woman carried was pointed backwards while the outer spears were pointed forward.

Both voiced the question of how they would be able to spear the bull?

The bull was quickly approaching the two young men when to their amazement both of the women increased their speed to run in front of the bull.

White Swan let out a loud, "Now" as she stepped ever so slightly in and planted the butt of the spear into the ground and placed the tip just inside the front leg of the bull.

Quite Pheasant did the right-hand opposite.

The two spears instantly killed the young bull who came to his knees less than a spears length from Grey Fox Running and Red Oak.

White Swan and Quite Pheasant let out their victory cry and did their round dance. Then they both turned to the two thoroughly amazed young men and in an exaggerated show, pointed to the bull.

"Will you teach us how to hunt like this," the two men asked in unison.

"We will only teach our mates," White Swan replied in a bold way.

She was, in fact, immediately afraid of the reply.

"I don't know what to say. They hunt well, but can they cook, and will they be able to wash off the smell of the sweat mixed with the blood of the buffalo? What do you think," Grey Fox Running replied as he turned to Red Oak?

"I think that we are out classed, out hunted and should concentrate on getting this buffalo skinned. I did notice a small spring back in the woods that will provide both water to drink and to wash off," Red Oak commented as he pulled out his skinning blade and once again looked at the two spears sticking into the chest of the young buffalo.

White Swan thanked Red Oak for mentioning the spring and then signaled to Quite Pheasant to follow her.

"You just asked Grey Fox Running to be your mate, but he did not answer, what now." Quiet Pheasant commented.

"I heard him say yes. He just wants me to smell better than a buffalo," White Swan said as she thought about the position, she had put him in.

You should ask Red Oak, White Swan continued with a chuckle.

White Swan's interpretation was a good one and Quiet Pheasant took her advice and proposed a similar union with Red Oak.

Later they were able to give a positive answer to their father's question.

"Will I be hunting for two mate-less daughters or was the hunt successful," their father asked on their return.

"Look at their faces and you will see your answer," their mother replied as she gave her two daughters a hug.

Quiet Pheasant commented that her shameless sister had extended the proposal to Grey Fox Running and that she had followed her older sister's lead and shamed Red Oak to make a mating proposal as well.

And then we gave the buffalo to the two young men so they could come by and gift our parents with the meat.

White Swan laughed and commented that the rest of the clan meeting would go slowly but she and her sister would be moving into a new clan and have two handsome warriors to hunt with.

THE END

Thank you for reading to this point!

About the Author

Ronald E. Mueller
remwriter95@gmail.com

Ron grew up in what is now Flint River State Park in Southeast Iowa. The 170-year-old house Ron lived in is built into a hillside. It faces a 125-foot-high cliff towering over the little Flint River. The house and the land talked to him about; the passing of time, the struggle to conquer the land, the struggles people faced and the wonder of nature.

He climbed the cliffs, crawled into the caves, dove from the swimming rock, collected clams from the bottom of the pond, gigged and skinned frogs for their legs. He trapped muskrats for fur, hunted raccoon in the dead of night, and with only a stick hunted rabbits in the dead of winter.

His young life was outdoors, and nature tested him.

He walked to a one room stone schoolhouse uphill both ways. A stern but warm-hearted teacher, Mrs. Henry was instrumental in shaping his character as she shepherded him from the fourth to the eighth grade.

It was a great way to grow up.

Ron graduated from Burlington, High School, went to Vietnam in the Navy. He graduated from The University of South Florida with a master's degree in engineering, worked for thirty eight years for Procter and Gamble, traveled around the world thirty times.

He has remained happily married for more than fifty years. His daughter and his two sons are all successful and his three grandchildren have all graduated.

His wife has humored and supported him as he became a full time professional story teller.

He has come to realize that he is, what is known as, a Cozy writer. Excitement and adventure but little guts and gore. His heroine or hero suffer a little but live happily ever after.

His experiences inter-twined with snippets of fantasy lend themselves to the adventures he leads the reader through.

Published by: Around the World Publishing, LLC.

https://www.remwriter95.net/